See you later, Alligator!

by
Annie Kubler

Child's Play (International) Ltd
Ashworth Rd, Bridgemead, Swindon SN5 7YD, UK
Swindon   Auburn ME   Sydney
ISBN 978-1-904550-05-1   HH310321FP0621051

Wake up,
Alligator!

We've got
a busy day ahead.
Lots to do!

I'm going shopping for some bread.

Are you coming, Alligator?

Not right now, Crocodile.

I must have a bath!

See you later, Alligator!

In a while, Crocodile!

Time to clean the house!

Will you help me, Alligator?

It's too early, Crocodile.

I haven't had breakfast yet!

See you later, Alligator!

In a while, Crocodile!

I have to hang the clothes out to dry.

Will you do your share, Alligator?

See you later, Alligator!

In a while, Crocodile!

I'm off to water the plants.

Will you give me a hand, Alligator?

Not yet, Crocodile.

I must finish my book first!

See you later, Alligator!

In a while, Crocodile!

I'm going to catch my lunch.

Will you join in, Alligator?

Sorry Crocodile, I'm busy.

I must get on with my painting!

In a while, Crocodile!